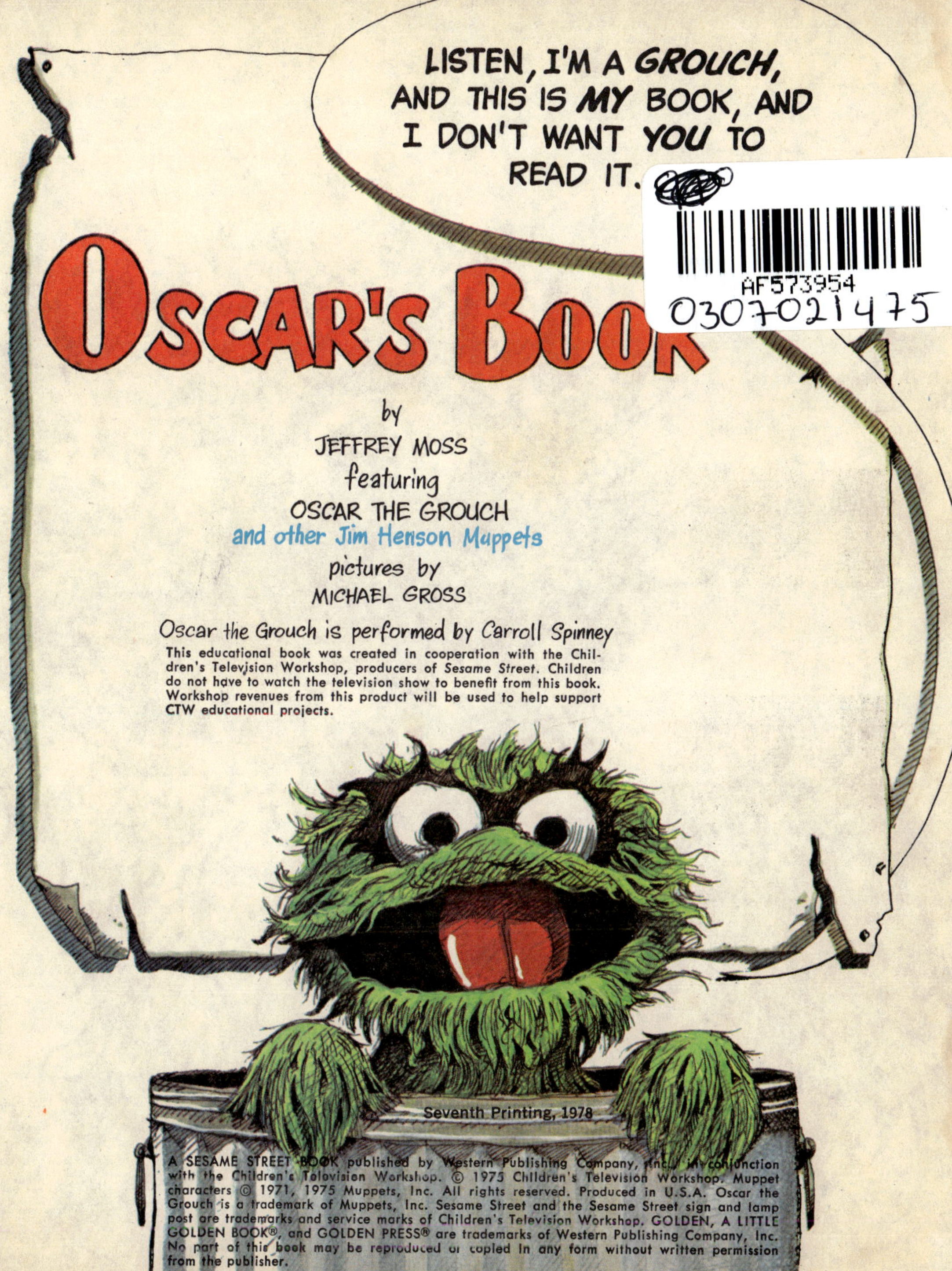

OSCAR'S BOOK

by
JEFFREY MOSS
featuring
OSCAR THE GROUCH
and other Jim Henson Muppets
pictures by
MICHAEL GROSS

Oscar the Grouch is performed by Carroll Spinney

This educational book was created in cooperation with the Children's Television Workshop, producers of *Sesame Street*. Children do not have to watch the television show to benefit from this book. Workshop revenues from this product will be used to help support CTW educational projects.

Seventh Printing, 1978

A SESAME STREET BOOK published by Western Publishing Company, Inc., in conjunction with the Children's Television Workshop.

HEY! WHO SAID YOU COULD COME SO CLOSE TO ME? I WANT TO PLAY WITH MY TRASH, AND I WANT YOU FAR, FAR AWAY!

GOOD! NOW YOU'RE *FAR* AWAY FROM ME, AND I CAN PLAY WITH MY WONDERFUL, YUCCHY TRASH!

HEY! YOU CAME *CLOSE* AGAIN! OKAY, IF THAT'S THE WAY YOU'RE GOING TO BE—YOU KNOW WHAT I'M GOING TO DO? I'M GOING TO MOVE OUT OF THIS TRASH CAN AND LET SOMEBODY ELSE MOVE IN!

HELLO, THERE. I'M A LITTLE GIRL, AND I LIVE IN THIS TRASH CAN. MY NAME IS MELODY. OSCAR THE GROUCH DOESN'T LIVE HERE ANY MORE, SO I GUESS EVERYBODY WILL HAVE TO FIND SOMEONE ELSE TO BOTHER.... OH-OH. HERE COMES SOMEBODY.

OH, LOOK! THERE'S A NEW LITTLE GIRL IN OUR NEIGHBORHOOD!
HEY, EVERYBODY! COME MEET THE NEW LITTLE GIRL ON SESAME STREET!
OH, NO!

ALL RIGHT, ALL RIGHT! I WAS JUST PRETENDING! THERE'S NO LITTLE GIRL HERE. SEE? IT'S ME, OSCAR! NOW WILL EVERYBODY LEAVE ME ALONE?

OKAY, I'VE HAD IT! NOW YOU'LL NEVER SEE ME AGAIN. I'M GOING TO DO SOMETHING SO YOU'LL NEVER BE ABLE TO FIND ME!

NOW NO ONE WILL EVER FIND ME! HEH-HEH!

WHAT DO YOU MEAN, YOU CAN SEE ME?

OKAY, SO YOU CAN SEE ME. SO WHAT? I'VE GOT ANOTHER IDEA! I'VE GOT THE BIGGEST AND BEST WAY EVER TO KEEP PEOPLE FROM BOTHERING ME.

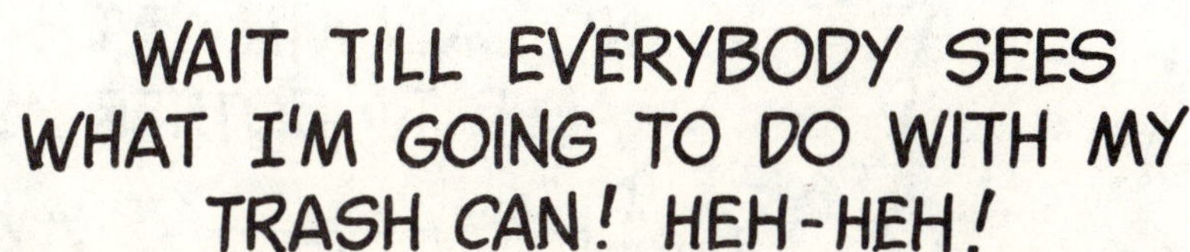
WAIT TILL EVERYBODY SEES WHAT I'M GOING TO DO WITH MY TRASH CAN! HEH-HEH!

HERE IT IS — THE SUPERDUPER GROUCH ROCKET BALLOON, DESIGNED TO TAKE ME UP INTO THE SKY, WHERE NO ONE WILL EVER BE ABLE TO BOTHER ME!

UP I GO!
AWAY FROM EVERYBODY!
FANTASTIC! GOOD-BYE
FOREVER!

BOY, IT'S REALLY TERRIFIC UP HERE!

HEY, WAIT A MINUTE! WHAT'S THAT DUMB LITTLE BIRD DOING?

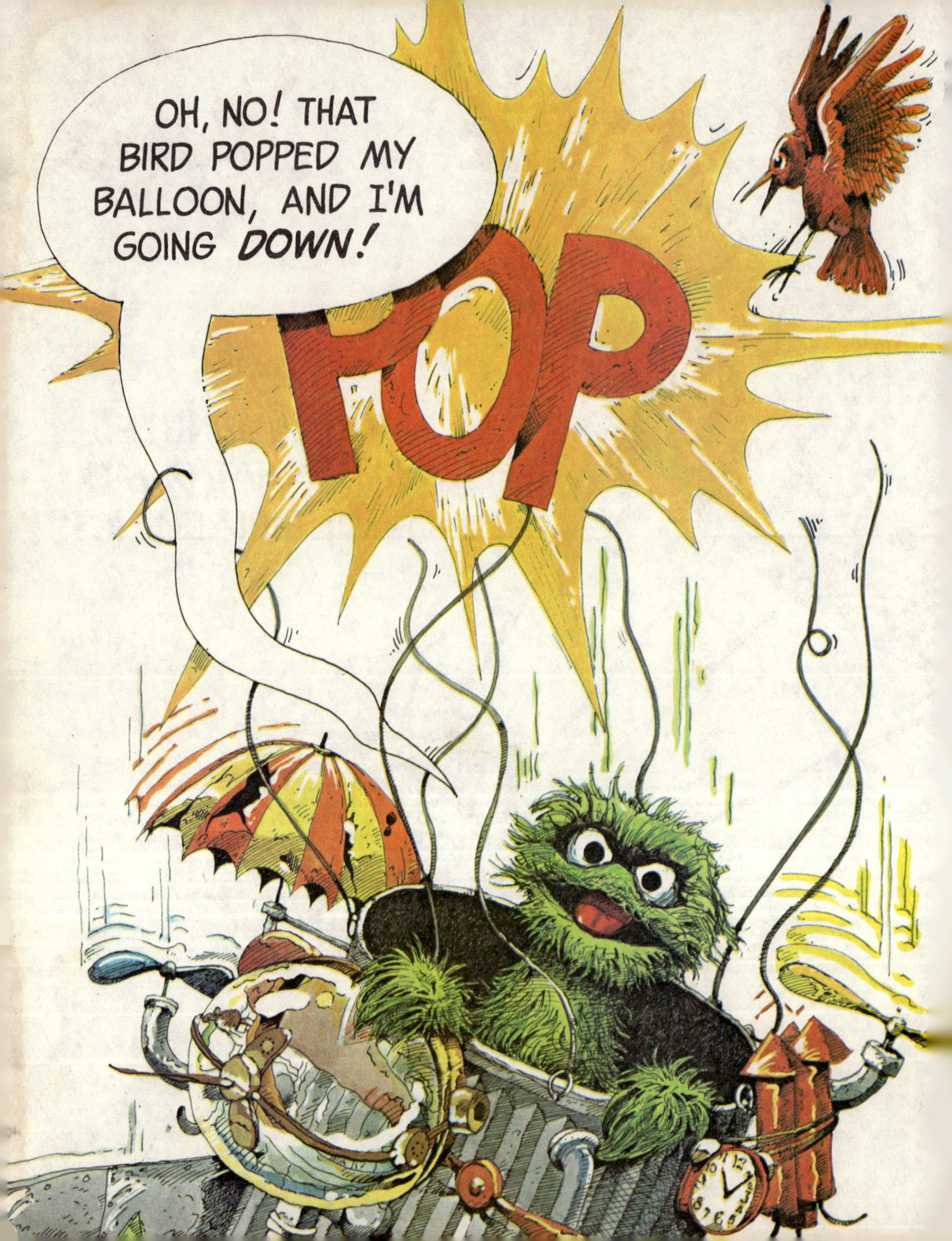
OH, NO! THAT BIRD POPPED MY BALLOON, AND I'M GOING *DOWN*!
POP

ARE YOU STILL READING THIS BOOK? CAN'T I ***EVER*** GET YOU TO GO AWAY? HEY, I'VE GOT AN IDEA. DO YOU KNOW THE DIFFERENCE BETWEEN ***OPEN*** AND ***CLOSED?*** WELL, NOW YOUR EYES ARE ***OPEN***. SEE IF YOU CAN ***CLOSE*** YOUR EYES REALLY TIGHT, AND KEEP THEM CLOSED WHILE YOU TURN THE PAGE.

HA! NOW
YOUR EYES ARE CLOSED,
AND YOU CAN'T SEE
ME, AND THAT'S HOW
I LIKE IT!

HEY!
WHO SAID YOU COULD
OPEN YOUR EYES?

BOY, YOU'RE REALLY SOMETHING! FIRST I DISGUISED MYSELF; THEN I TRIED TO HIDE FROM YOU; THEN I BUILT MY SUPER-DUPER GROUCH ROCKET BALLOON; AND THEN I TRICKED YOU INTO CLOSING YOUR EYES. NOW THIS BOOK IS ALMOST OVER, AND I STILL CAN'T GET YOU TO...

HEY, WAIT A MINUTE!
THIS IS THE *END* OF THIS
BOOK! WHEN YOU CLOSE THE BOOK,
I WON'T HAVE ANYBODY TO COMPLAIN
TO. I *LIKE* YELLING AND COMPLAINING,
SO DON'T CLOSE THIS BOOK!...
HEY, COME BACK HERE!... YOU
REALLY MAKE ME *MAD!*...